SEE YOU ON THE TRAIL—

2009

GLACIER PARK WIDE

Montana is big sky country.
The big sky meets big landscape in Glacier National Park.

The park visitor is often disappointed upon the return home because their snapshots incompletely capture the memory of dramatic vistas imprinted on the mind. This collection of wide format photographs is an expression of the desire to replicate the personal encounter with this remarkable place.

Look at the pictures.
Listen to the water.
Feel the wind.
Smell the cedar.
Remember the time when your senses were on overload . . . . and enjoy!

Tom Esch

 "CONTINENTAL DIVIDE"   CONTINENTAL DIVIDE FROM MT. BROWN LOOKOUT, 2008

Glacier Park Wide is a dialogue through one man's eyes expressing the vast freedom found in the wide open spaces of the West. For Bret Bouda, the author of "Glacier Classics", black and white centennial book of Glacier National Park, English is his seventh language but the images (24" x 7" panoramic views) in his book transcend words. Escaping Communist Czechoslovakia, Bret came to America in search of freedom. In this book (and in most of his other photography work), he uses the lens of his camera to convey that freedom. Regardless of language or culture, this book imparts a profound message of beauty. It is the perfect keepsake for now and generations to come, attesting to the natural treasures comprising this spectacular region of the world.

Digital Broadway Publishing LLC
PO Box 1833, Kalispell - MT 59903

www.digitalbroadwaypublishing.com

Bret Bouda
Photography, Glacier Park Wide

ISBN # 978-1-60743-133-6

First Edition

Printed in USA

 "LAKE MC DONALD" LAKE MCDONALD & LIVINGSTON RANGE VIEW FROM APGAR VILLAGE, 2008

"SIYEH PASS" VIEW FROM SIYEH PASS AT SEXTON GLACIER BELOW GOING-TO-THE-SUN MOUNTAIN, 2008

"BIRD WOMAN FALLS"   BIRD WOMAN FALLS FALLING DOWN MT. OBERLIN, 2008

 "PITAMAKAN PASS TRAIL"   LEWIS RANGE MOUNTAIN VIEW FROM THE PITAMAKAN/DAWSON PASSES TRAIL, 2007

"HEAVENS PEAK MOUNTAIN" VIEW AT HEAVENS PEAK FROM MUCH OF THE GOING-TO-THE-SUN ROAD, 2008

"PITAMAKAN / DAWSON PASSES"   VIEW AT PITAMAKAN (LEFT) AND DAWSON (RIGHT) PASSES , 2007

 "BEAVER CHIEF FALLS"   CASCADES FROM LAKE ELLEN WILSON TO LINCOLN LAKE, 2007

"LAKE MC DONALD"   LAKE MCDONALD FROM MT. BROWN LOOKOUT, 2008

 "CUT BANK VALLEY" CUT BANK VALLEY OF GLACIER NATIONAL PARK, 2008

 "MARIAS PASS"   CROSSING THE LEWIS RANGE OF THE CONTINENTAL DIVIDE - 5213 FT, 2008

 "THE GARDEN WALL" THE CONTINENTAL DIVIDE BETWEN LOGAN AND SWFTCURRENT PASSES , 2008

 "ICEBERG LAKE & PTARMIGAN WALL"   PTARMIGAN WALL RANGE, 2008

"FLORAL PARK"   THE BACKCOUNTRY OF GLACIER NATIONAL PARK, 2007

 "BIG PRAIRIE / POLEBRIDGE" THE BIG PRAIRIE ON THE BANKS OF THE NORTH FORK RIVER, 2007

"MANY GLACIER HOTEL"   LARGEST HOTEL IN THE PARK - MANY GLACIER HOTEL, 2007

 "MOUNT CLEMENS" MEADOW WITH WILDFLOWERS BELOW MT. CLEMENS FROM LOGAN PASS VISITOR CENTER, 2008

 "GUNSIGHT LAKE"   GUNSIGHT LAKE IN THE ST. MARY VALLEY, GUNSIGHT PASS IN BACKGROUND, 2007

 "HAYSTACK FALLS"   HAYSTACK FALLS ON GOING-TO-THE-SUN ROAD, 2008

"AVALANCHE CREEK"   AVALANCHE CREEK, BLUE COLORED WATER CAUSED BY GLACIAL SILT, 2008

"LOGAN PASS"   LOGAN PASS VISITOR CENTER, 2008

44

Many years ago, a young Piegan warrior was noted for his bravery. When he grew older and more experienced in war, he became the war-chief for a large band of Piegan warriors. A little while after he became the war-chief, he fell in love with a girl who was in his tribe, and they got married. He was so in love with her that he took no other wives, and he decided not to go on war parties anymore. He and his wife were very happy together; unusually so, and when they had a baby, they were even happier then. Some moons later, a war party that had left his village was almost destroyed by an enemy. Only four men came back to tell the story. The war-chief was greatly troubled by this. He saw that if the enemy was not punished, they would raid the Piegan camp. So he gave a big war feast and asked all of the young men of his band to come to it. After they had all eaten their fill, the war-chief arose and said to them in solemn tones: "Friends and brothers, you have all heard the story that our four young men have told us. All the others who went out from our camp were killed by the enemy. Only these four have come back to our campfires. Those who were killed were our friends and relatives. "We who live must go out on the warpath to avenge the fallen. If we don't, the enemy will think that we are weak and that they can attack us unhurt. Let us not let them attack us here in the camp. "I will lead a party on the warpath. Who here will go with me against the enemy that has killed our friends and brothers?" A party of brave warriors gathered around him, willing to follow their leader. His wife also asked to join the party, but he told her to stay at the camp. "If you go without me," she said, "you will find an empty lodge when you return." The Chief talked to her and calmed her, and finally convinced her to stay with the women and children and old men in the camp at the foot of a high mountain. Leading a large party of men, the Chief rode out from the village. The Piegans met the enemy and defeated them. But their war-chief was killed. Sadly, his followers carried the broken body back to the camp.

His wife was crazed with grief. With vacant eyes she wandered everywhere, looking for her husband and calling his name. Her friends took care of her, hoping that eventually her mind would become clear again and that she could return to normal life. One day, though, they could not find her anywhere in the campe. Searching for her, they saw her high up on the side of the mountain, the tall one above their camp. She had her baby in her arms. The head man of the village sent runners after her, but from the top of the mountain she signalled that they should not try to reach her. All watched in horror as she threw her baby out over the cliff, and then herself jumped from the mountain to the rocks far, far below. Her people buried the woman and baby there among the rocks. They carried the body of the Chief to the place and buried him beside them. From that time on, the mountain that towers above the graves was known as Minnow Stahkoo, "the Mountain of the Chief", or "Chief Mountain".

If you look closely, even today, you can see on the face of the mountain the figure of a woman with a baby inn her arms, the wife and child of the Chief.

"CHIEF MOUNTAIN"   RISING ABRUPTLY OUT OF THE NORTHERN PLAINS CHIEF MOUNTAIN IS A MOST IMPRESSIVE TOWER,

CHIEF MOUNTAIN
a story from Blackfoot Stories
and Legends...

 **"OLD MAN LAKE"** OLD MAN LAKE UNDER PITAMAKAN PASS, 2007

"SAINT MARY LAKE" SAINT MARY LAKE WITH CONTINENTAL DIVIDE IN BACKGROUND FROM HWY 89, 2008

"HEAVENS PEAK MOUNTAIN" DOMINATING VIEW AT HEAVENS PEAK FROM THE AIR, MT. CLEVELAND ON RIGHT, 2008

 "LAKE McDONALD"   SUNRISE AT LAKE MCDONALD , 2004

 "SWIFTCURRENT LOOKOUT"   EXTENSIVE VIEW FROM SWIFTCURRENT LOOKOUT ON THE CONTINENTAL DIVIDE, 2007

 "HIGHLINE TRAIL" DOMINATING VIEW AT HEAVENS PEAK (LAKE MCDONALD ON LEFT) FROM THE HIGHLINE TRAIL, 2008

"SWIFTCURRENT TRAIL"   BURNED FOREST ALONG SWFTCURRENT TRAIL, 2008

 "MANY GLACIER"   EARLY MORNING VIEW AT MANY GLACIER HOTEL ON SWIFTCURRENT LAKE, 2008

"CUT BANK"   CUT BANK RIDGE FROM HWY 89, 2008

 "LAKE MC DONALD"   FROZEN LAKE MCDONALD, 2007

 "LOWER ST MARY LAKE"   LOWER SAINT MARY LAKE VIEW FROM HWY 89, 2008

"AVALANCHE LAKE"   EARLY MORNING AT AVALANCHE LAKE, 2008

"CONTINENTAL DIVIDE"   LEWIS AND CLARK RANGE - CONTINENTAL DIVIDE, 2008

 "LOWER TWO MEDICINE LAKE" LOWER TWO MEDICINE LAKE IN FRONT OF CONTINENTAL DIVIDE, 2008

"THE TRAIL OF THE CEDARS"   THE TRAIL OF THE CEDARS AT THE AVALANCHE CREEK AREA IS A BEAUTIFUL WALK, 2008

"BOWMAN LAKE"   VIEW FROM NUMA RIDGE AT BOWMAN LAKE AND RAINBOW PEAK , 2008

"LAKE SHERBURNE" MANY GLACIER PARK ENTRANCE AT LAKE SHERBURNE, 2008

"FLORAL PARK PASS"   AVALANCHE LAKE (LEFT) AND HIDDEN LAKE FROM FLORAL PARK PASS, 2007

"THE LOOP"   VIEW AT THE LOGAN PASS FROM THE LOOP (GOING-TO-THE-SUN ROAD), 2008

 "GOING-TO-THE-SUN ROAD" EAST SIDE VIEWS FROM GOING-TO-THE-SUN ROAD, 2008

 "SPERRY GLACIER BASIN" FLORAL PARK PASS AND CONTINENTAL DIVIDE FROM SPERRY GLACIER BASIN, 2007

 "BOWMAN LAKE" RAINBOW PEAK (RIGHT) AND NUMA PEAK FROM BOWMAN LAKE , 2008

 **"SIYEH PASS"**   EAST VIEW FROM SIYEH PASS , 2008

"GRANITE PARK CHALET"   LEWIS AND CLARK RANGE FROM GRANITE PARK (SWIFTCURRENT TRAIL), 2007

HISTORY

ESTABLISHED AS A PARK ON MAY 11, 1910.
ESTABLISHED AS WATERTON-GLACIER INTERNATIONAL PEACE PARK IN 1932.
GOING- TO- THE-SUN ROAD COMPLETED IN 1932.
ESTABLISHED AS AN INTERNATIONAL BIOSPHERE RESERVE, 1974.
WATERTON LAKES NATIONAL PARK ESTABLISHED IN 1895.
ESTABLISHED AS WATERTON-GLACIER INTERNATIONAL PEACE PARK WORLD HERITAGE SITE, 1995.

FACILITIES

NUMBER CLASS A CAMPGROUNDS: 8, WITH 943 SITES
NUMBER CLASS B CAMPGROUNDS: 5, WITH 61 SITES
NUMBER OF TRAILS: 151; TOTAL LENGTH - 743.3 MILES
MILES OF CONTINENTAL DIVIDE TRAIL IN GLACIER: 106

"WEST GLACIER"   WEST GLACIER (WEST ENTRANCE) FROM HWY 2, 2008

WATER

TOTAL NUMBER OF LAKES: 762
MILES OF SHORELINE: 392
LARGEST LAKE: LAKE MCDONALD (9.4 MILES LONG; 1.5 MILES WIDE; 464 FEET DEEP; 6,823 ACRES)
NUMBER OF STREAMS: 563
LONGEST STREAM: UPPER MCDONALD CREEK (25.8 MILES)
TOTAL MILES OF STREAMS INSIDE THE PARK: 2,865 MILES

LAND

ACREAGE: 1,013,594 ACRES...500+ IN PRIVATE OWNERSHIP
SQUARE MILES: 1,583
MILES OF EXTERIOR BOUNDARY: 205
SHARED WITH WATERTON NATIONAL PARK: 21 MILES
SHARED WITH BRITISH COLUMBIA: 31 MILES
SHARED WITH U.S. FOREST SERVICE: 130 MILES